On Top!

by Mickey Daronco

I got my tan cot.

I put it up. Then I got on top of my cot. I will have a nap on it.

Look at my big pup.

It can sit on my bed.

I can get on top of it!

Look at this.

I got it for me.

Then I got on top of it!

Look at me.

I have a mop.

I got on my mop!